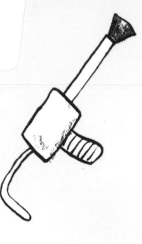

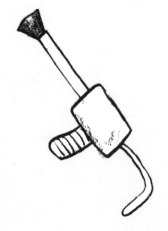

HORRiD HENRY'S
Fearsome
Four

There are many more
Horrid Henry Early Readers available.
For a complete list,
visit www.horridhenry.co.uk
or www.orionbooks.co.uk.

Francesca Simon

HORRiD HENRY'S Fearsome Four

Illustrated by Tony Ross

Orion
Children's Books

This collection first published in Great Britain in 2012
by Orion Children's Books
a division of the Orion Publishing Group Ltd
Orion House
5 Upper St Martin's Lane
London WC2H 9EA
An Hachette UK Company

1 3 5 7 9 10 8 6 4 2

A catalogue record for this book is available from the British Library.

ISBN 978 1 4440 0657 5

Printed in China

www.orionbooks.co.uk
www.horridhenry.co.uk

Contents

HORRID HENRY'S
Birthday Party

Contents

To my agent, Rosemary Sandberg,
with grateful thanks

Chapter 1

February was Horrid Henry's
favourite month.
His birthday was in February.

"It's my birthday soon!" said Henry
every day after Christmas.

"And my birthday party! Hurray!"

February was Horrid Henry's parents' least favourite month.

"It's Henry's birthday soon,"
said Dad, groaning.

"And his birthday party," said Mum,
groaning even louder.

Every year they thought Henry's
birthday parties could not get worse.
But they always did.

Every year Henry's parents said they
would never ever let Henry have
a birthday party again.
But every year they gave Henry
one absolutely last final chance.

Henry had big plans for this
year's party.

"I want to go to Lazer Zap,"
said Henry. He'd been to Lazer Zap
for Tough Toby's party. They'd had a
great time dressing up as spacemen
and blasting each other in dark
tunnels all afternoon.

"NO!" said Mum. "Too violent."
"I agree," said Dad.
"And too expensive," said Mum.
"I agree," said Dad.

There was a moment's silence.

"However," said Dad, "it does mean
the party wouldn't be here."

Mum looked at Dad.
Dad looked at Mum.
"How do I book?" said Mum.

"Hurray!" shrieked Henry.

ZAP!

ZAP!

ZAP!

Chapter 2

Horrid Henry sat in his fort holding
a pad of paper. On the front cover in
big capital letters Henry wrote:

HENRY'S
PARTY PLANS

TOP SECRET!!!!

At the top of the first page Henry
had written:

Guests

A long list followed.
Then Henry stared at the names
and chewed his pencil.

Actually, I don't
want Margaret,
thought Henry.
Too moody.
He crossed out
Moody Margaret's
name.

Margaret

Susan

And I definitely
don't want Susan.
Too crabby.

In fact, I don't want any girls at all,
thought Henry.

Clare

He crossed out
Clever Clare

and Lazy Linda.

Linda

21

Then there was Anxious Andrew.

Nope, thought
Henry, crossing
him off.
He's no fun.

Andrew

Toby

Toby was
possible, but
Henry didn't
really like him.
Out went
Tough Toby.

William?
No way, thought
Henry. He'll be
crying the second
he gets zapped.
Out went Weepy
William.

william

Ralph?
Henry considered.
Ralph would be
good because he was
sure to get into trouble.
On the other hand,
he hadn't invited Henry to *his* party.

Ralph

Rude Ralph was struck off.

So were
Babbling Bob,
Jolly Josh,

Bob

Josh

Greedy Graham
and Dizzy Dave.

Graham

Dave

24

And absolutely no way was
Peter coming anywhere near him
on his birthday.

Peter

Ahh, that was better. No horrid kids
would be coming to *his* party.

There was only one problem.
Every single name was crossed off.
No guests meant no presents.

Henry looked at his list. Margaret
was a moody old grouch and he
hated her, but she did sometimes
give good gifts. He still had the
jumbo box of day-glo slime she'd
given him last year.

And Toby *had* invited Henry
to *his* party.

And Dave was always spinning round
like a top, falling and knocking things
over which was fun. Graham would
eat too much and burp.

And Ralph was sure to say
rude words and make all the
grown-ups angry.

Oh, let them all come,
thought Henry. Except Peter,
of course. The more guests I have,
the more presents I get!

Henry turned to the next page
and wrote:

PRESENTS I WANT

Super Soaker 2000,
the best water blaster ever

Spy Fax

Micro Machines

Slime

Inter-galactic Samurai Gorillas

Stink bombs

Pet rats

Whoopee cushion

25-gear mountain bike

Money

He'd leave the list lying around
where Mum and Dad were sure
to find it.

Chapter 3

"I've done the menu for the party," said Mum. "What do you think?"

MUM'S MENU

carrot sticks

cucumber sandwiches

peanut butter sandwiches

grapes

raisins

apple juice

carrot cake

"Blecccccch," said Henry. "I don't want that horrible food at my party. I want food that I like."

Henry's Menu

Pickled Onion Monster Munch
Smoky Spider Shreddies
Super Spicy Hedgehog Crisps
Crunchy Crackles
Twizzle Fizzle Sticks
Purple Planet-buster Drink
chocolate bars
chocolate eggs
Chocolate Monster Cake

"You can't just have junk food,"
said Mum.
"It's not junk food," said Henry.
"Crisps are made from potatoes,
and Monster Munch has onions –
that's two vegetables."

"Henry . . ." said Mum.
She looked fierce.

Henry looked at his menu. Then he
added, in small letters at the bottom:

peanut butter sandwiches

"But only in the middle of the table,"
said Henry. "So no one has to eat
them who doesn't want them."

"All right," said Mum.
Years of fighting with Henry about
his parties had worn her down.

"And Peter's not coming,"
said Henry.

"What?!" said Perfect Peter, looking
up from polishing his shoes.

"Peter is your brother. Of course
he's invited."

Henry
scowled.
"But he'll ruin
everything."

"No Peter, no party," said Mum.

Henry pretended
he was a fire-
breathing dragon.

"**Owww!**" shrieked Peter.

Don't be horrid,
Henry!

"All right,"
said Henry.
"He can come. But you'd better keep
out of my way," he hissed at Peter.

"Mum!" wailed Peter.
"Henry's being mean to me."

"Stop it, Henry," said Mum.

Henry decided to change the
subject fast. "What about party bags?"
said Henry.

"I want everyone to have Slime, and loads and loads and loads of sweets! Dirt Balls, Nose Pickers and Foam Teeth are the best."

"We'll see," said Mum. She looked at the calendar. Only two more days. Soon it would be over.

Chapter 4

Henry's birthday arrived at last.

"Happy birthday, Henry!" said Peter.
"Where are my presents?"
said Henry.

Dad pointed. Horrid Henry
attacked the pile.

Mum and Dad
had given him
a First
Encyclopaedia,
Scrabble,
a fountain pen,
a hand-knitted
cardigan,
a globe, and
three sets of
vests and pants.

"Oh," said Henry. He pushed the
dreadful presents aside.

"Anything else?" he asked hopefully.
Maybe they were keeping the
Super Soaker for last.
"I've got a present for you," said
Peter. "I chose it myself."
Henry tore off the wrapping paper.
It was a tapestry kit.

"Yuck!"

"I'll have it if you don't want it,"
said Peter.
"No!" said Henry, snatching
up the kit.

"Wasn't it a great idea to have Henry's
party at Lazer Zap?" said Dad.
"Yes," said Mum. "No mess, no fuss."
They smiled at each other.

Ring   ring.

Dad answered the phone.
It was the Lazer Zap lady.
"Hello! I was just ringing to check
the birthday boy's name," she said.
"We like to announce it over our
loudspeaker during the party."

Dad gave Henry's name.
A terrible scream came from the
other end of the phone. Dad held
the receiver away from his ear.

The shrieking and screaming
continued.

"Hmmmn," said Dad. "I see. Thank
you." Dad hung up. He looked pale.

"Is it true that you wrecked the
place when you went to Lazer Zap
with Toby?" said Dad.
"No!" said Henry.
He tried to look harmless.
"And trampled on several children?"

"No!" said Henry.
"Yes you did," said Perfect Peter.

"And what about all the lasers you broke?"

"What lasers?" said Henry.

"And the slime you put in the space suits?" said Peter.

"That wasn't me, telltale," shrieked Henry. "What about my party?"

"I'm afraid Lazer Zap
have banned you," said Dad.

"But what about Henry's party?"
said Mum. She looked pale.

"But what about my party?!" wailed
Henry. "I want to go to Lazer Zap!"

"Never mind," said Dad brightly.
"I know lots of good games."

Chapter 5

Ding dong.

It was the first guest, Sour Susan.
She held a large present.
Henry snatched the package.

It was a pad of paper and
some felt tip pens.
"How lovely," said Mum.
"What do you say, Henry?"
"I've already got that," said Henry.

Don't be
horrid, Henry!

I don't care, thought Henry.
This was the worst day of his life.

Ding dong.

It was the second guest, Anxious
Andrew. He held a tiny present.
Henry snatched the package.
"It's awfully small," said Henry, tearing
off the wrapping. "And it smells."

It was a box of animal soaps.

"How super," said Dad.
"What do you say, Henry?"

Ugghhh!

Don't be horrid,
Henry!

Henry stuck out his lower lip.
"It's my party and I'll do what
I want," muttered Henry.

"Watch your step, young man,"
said Dad.
Henry stuck out his tongue
behind Dad's back.

More guests arrived.

Lazy Linda gave him a "Read and
Listen" CD of favourite fairy tales:
Cinderella, Snow White,
and Sleeping Beauty.

"Fabulous," said Mum.

"Yuck!"

said Henry.

Clever Clare handed him
a square package.

Henry held it by the corners.
"It's a book," he groaned.

"My favourite present!" said Peter.
"Wonderful," said Mum.
"What is it?"
Henry unwrapped it slowly.

COOK YOUR OWN
HEALTHY
NUTRITIOUS FOOD

"Great!" said Perfect Peter.
"Can I borrow it?"

"**NO!**" screamed Henry.
Then he threw the book on the floor
and stomped on it.

"Henry!" hissed Mum. "I'm warning
you. When someone gives you a
present you say thank you."

Rude Ralph was the last to arrive. He handed Henry a long rectangular package wrapped in newspaper.

It was a Super Soaker 2000 water blaster.

"Oh,"
said Mum.

"Put it away,"
said Dad.

"Thank you, Ralph," beamed Henry.
"Just what I wanted."

Chapter 6

"Let's start with Pass the Parcel,"
said Dad.
"I hate Pass the Parcel,"
said Horrid Henry.
What a horrible party this was.

"I love Pass the Parcel," said
Perfect Peter.

"I don't want
to play," said
Sour Susan.

"When do
we eat?" said
Greedy Graham.

Dad started the music.
"Pass the parcel, William," said Dad.

"No!"

shrieked William. "It's mine!"
"But the music is still playing,"
said Dad.
William burst into tears.
Horrid Henry tried to snatch
the parcel.

Dad stopped the music.

William stopped crying instantly
and tore off the wrapping.
"A granola bar," he said.

"That's a
terrible
prize," said
Rude Ralph.

"Is it my turn yet?"
said Anxious Andrew.

"When do we eat?"
said Greedy Graham.

"I hate Pass the Parcel,"
screamed Henry.
"I want to play
something else."

"Musical Statues!"
announced Mum brightly.

"You're out, Henry,"
said Dad.
"You moved."

"I didn't," said Henry.

"Yes you did," said Toby.

"No, I didn't," said Henry.
"I'm not leaving."

"That's not fair,"
shrieked Sour Susan.

"I'm not
playing," whined
Dizzy Dave.

"I'm tired,"
sulked Lazy Linda.

"I hate Musical Statues,"
moaned Moody Margaret.

"Where's my prize?" demanded
Rude Ralph.
"A bookmark?" said Ralph.
"That's it?"

"Tea time!" said Dad.

The children pushed and shoved
their way to the table, grabbing and
snatching at the food.

"I hate fizzy drinks,"
said Tough Toby.

"I feel sick," said Greedy Graham.

"Where are the carrot sticks?"
said Perfect Peter.

Horrid Henry sat at the head
of the table. He didn't feel like
throwing food at Clare.
He didn't feel like rampaging with
Toby and Ralph. He didn't even feel
like kicking Peter.
He wanted to be at Lazer Zap.

Then Henry had a wonderful,
spectacular idea. He got up and
sneaked out of the room.

"Party bags," said Dad.

"What's in them?" said Tough Toby.
"Seedlings," said Mum.
"Where are the sweets?"
said Greedy Graham.
"This is the worst party bag
I've ever had," said Rude Ralph.

There was a noise outside.
Then Henry burst into the kitchen,
Super Soaker in hand.

shrieked Henry, drenching everyone
with water. "Ha! Ha! Gotcha!"

Splat went the cake.

Splash
went the drinks.

"EEEEEEEEEEEEEEKKK!"
shrieked the sopping wet children.

"HENRY!!!!"
yelled Mum
and Dad.

"YOU HORRID BOY!"
yelled Mum.
Water dripped from her hair.
"GO TO YOUR ROOM!"

"THIS IS YOUR LAST
PARTY EVER!" yelled Dad.
Water dripped from his clothes.

But Henry didn't care.
They said that every year.

HORRID HENRY'S
Underpants

Contents

For my nephew,
Jesse Benedek Simon

Chapter 1

A late birthday present! Whoopee!
Just when you thought you'd got
all your loot, more treasure arrives.
Horrid Henry shook the small
thin package.

It was light. Very light. Maybe it was
– oh, please let it be . . .

MONEY! Of course it was money.
What else could it be?

There was so much stuff he needed:

a Mutant Max lunchbox,

a Rapper Zapper Blaster,

and, of course,
the new Terminator Gladiator game
he kept seeing advertised on TV.

Mum and Dad were so mean and
horrible, they wouldn't buy it for
him. But he could buy whatever he
liked with his own money. So there.
Ha ha ha ha ha.

Wouldn't Ralph be green with envy
when he swaggered into school with
a Mutant Max lunchbox? And no
way would he even let Peter touch
his Rapper Zapper Blaster.

So how much money had he been
sent? Maybe enough for him to buy
everything! Horrid Henry tore off
the wrapping paper.

Aaaaarrrggghhhhh!

Great–Aunt Greta had done it again.

Great-Aunt Greta thought he was a girl. Great-Aunt Greta had been told ten billion times that his name was Henry, not Henrietta, and that he wasn't four years old.

But every year Peter would get £10,
or a football, or a computer game,
and Henry would get a Walkie-
Talkie-Teasy-Weasy-Burpy-Slurpy
Doll. Or a Princess Pamper Parlour.
Or Baby Poopie Pants.

And now this.

Horrid Henry picked up the birthday card. Maybe there was money inside. He opened it.

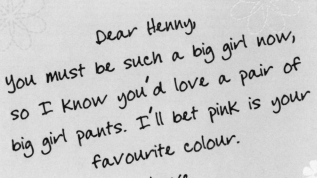

Dear Henny,
You must be such a big girl now, so I know you'd love a pair of big girl pants. I'll bet pink is your favourite colour.
Love,
Great Aunt Greta

Horrid Henry stared in horror at the
frilly pink lacy knickers, decorated
with glittery hearts and bows.

This was the worst present
he had ever received.

Worse than socks.

Worse than handkerchiefs.

Even worse
than a book.

Bleccccch! Ick! Yuck!

Horrid Henry chucked the hideous
underpants in the bin where they
belonged.

Ding dong.

Oh no!

Rude Ralph was here to play. If he
saw those knickers Henry would
never hear the end of it. His name
would be mud for ever.

Clump clump clump.

Ralph was stomping up the stairs to
his bedroom.

Henry snatched the terrible pants
from the bin and looked around his
room wildly for a hiding place.

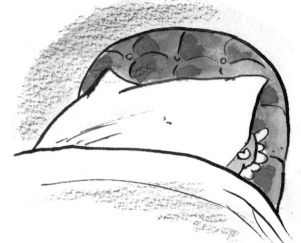

Under the pillow? What if they had
a pillow fight?

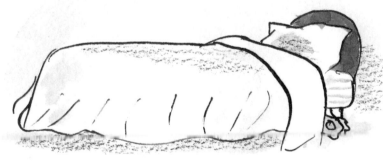

Under the bed? What if they
played hide and seek?

Quickly Henry stuffed them in the back of his pants drawer. I'll get rid of them the moment Ralph leaves, he thought.

Chapter 2

"Mercy, Your Majesty, mercy!"

King Henry the Horrible looked
down at his snivelling brother.
"Off with his head!" he ordered.

"Henry! Henry! Henry!" cheered his
grateful subjects.

"HENRY!"

King Henry the Horrible woke up.
His Medusa mother was looming
above him.

"You've overslept!" shrieked Mum.
"School starts in five minutes!
Get dressed! Quick! Quick!"
She pulled the duvet off Henry.
"Wha-wha?" mumbled Henry.

Dad raced into the room.
"Hurry!" shouted Dad. "We're late!"
He yanked Henry out of bed.

Henry stumbled around his dark
bedroom. Half-asleep, he reached
inside his underwear drawer, grabbed
a pair, then picked up some clothes
off the floor and flung everything on.
Then he, Dad, and Peter ran all the
way to school.

"Margaret! Stop pulling Susan's hair!"

"Ralph! Sit down!"

"Linda! Sit up!"

"Henry! Pay attention!" barked Miss Battle-Axe. "I am about to explain long division. I will only explain it once. You take a great big number, like 374, and then divide it—"

Horrid Henry was not paying
attention. He was tired. He was
crabby. And for some reason his
pants were itchy. These pants feel
horrible, he thought. And so tight.
What's wrong with them?

Horrid Henry sneaked a peek.
And then Horrid Henry saw what
pants he had on.

Not his Driller Cannibal pants.

Not his Marvin the Maniac ones either.

Not even his old Gross-Out ones,
with the holes and the droopy elastic.

He, Horrid Henry, was wearing frilly
pink lacy girls' pants covered in
glittery hearts and bows.

He'd completely forgotten he'd
stuffed them into his pants drawer last
month so Ralph wouldn't see them.
And now, oh horror of horrors,
he was wearing them.

Maybe it's a **nightmare**, thought
Horrid Henry hopefully.
He pinched his arm. Ouch! Then,
just to be sure, he pinched William.

"Waaaaah!" wailed Weepy William.

"Stop weeping, William!" said Miss Battle-Axe. "Now, what number do I need—"

It was not a **nightmare**. He was still in school, still wearing pink pants.

Chapter 3

What to do, what to do?

Don't panic,

thought Horrid Henry. He took
a deep breath. Don't panic.

After all, no one will know.
His trousers weren't see-through
or anything.

WAIT.

What trousers was he wearing? Were
there any holes in them? Quickly
Horrid Henry twisted round to
check his bottom.

Phew. There were no holes.
What luck he hadn't put on his old
jeans with the big rip, but a new pair.
He was safe.

"Henry! What's the answer?"
said Miss Battle-Axe.

"Pants," said Horrid Henry
before he could stop himself.

The class burst out laughing.

"Pants,"
screeched
Rude Ralph.

"Pants,"
screeched
Dizzy Dave.

"Henry. Stand up," ordered
Miss Battle-Axe.
Henry stood. His heart was
pounding.

The lacy ruffle of his pink pants
was showing!
His new trousers were too big.

Mum always bought him clothes that
were way too big so he'd grow into
them. These were the falling-down
ones he'd tried on yesterday.
Henry gripped his trousers tight
and yanked them up.

"What did you say?" said
Miss Battle-Axe slowly.

"Ants,"
said Horrid
Henry.

"Ants?"
said Miss Battle-Axe.

"Yeah," said Henry quickly. "I was
just thinking about how many ants
you could divide by – by that
number you said," he added.

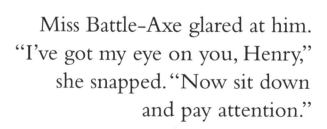

Miss Battle-Axe glared at him.
"I've got my eye on you, Henry,"
she snapped. "Now sit down
and pay attention."

Henry sat. All he had to do was tuck
in his T-shirt. That would keep his
trousers up. He'd look stupid but for
once Henry didn't care.

Just so long as no one ever knew
about his pink lacy pants.

And then Henry's blood turned
to ice. What was the latest craze
on the playground?

De-bagging.
Who'd started it?
Horrid Henry.
Yesterday he'd chased
Dizzy Dave and
pulled down his trousers.

The day before he'd
done the same thing
to Rude Ralph.

Just this morning he'd
de-bagged Tough Toby
on the way into class.
They'd all be trying
to de-bag him now.

I have to get another pair of pants,
thought Henry desperately.

Miss Battle-Axe passed round the
maths worksheets. Quickly Horrid
Henry scribbled down: 3, 7, 41, 174,
without reading any questions. He
didn't have time for long division.
Where could he find some other
pants? He could pretend to be sick
and get sent home from school.
But he'd already tried that twice
this week.

Wait. Wait. He was brilliant. He was a genius. What about Lost and Found? Someone, some time, must have lost some pants.

Chapter 4

Ding! Ding!

Before the playtime bell had finished
ringing Horrid Henry was out of his
seat and racing down the hall,
holding tight to his trousers.

He checked carefully to make sure
no one was watching, then he
ducked into Lost and Found. He'd
hide here until he found some pants.

The Lost and Found was stuffed with clothes. He rummaged through the mountains of

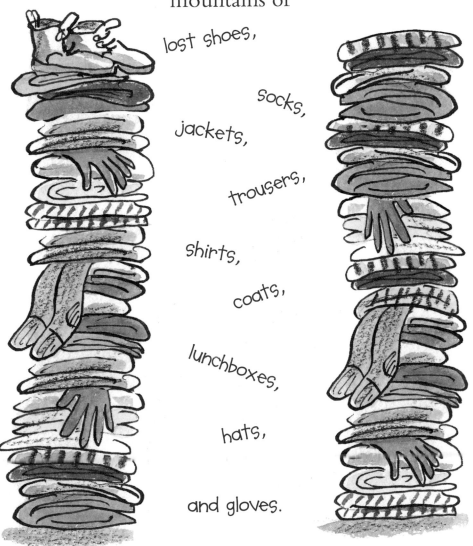

lost shoes,

socks,

jackets,

trousers,

shirts,

coats,

lunchboxes,

hats,

and gloves.

I'm amazed anyone leaves school wearing *anything*, thought Horrid Henry, tossing another sweatshirt over his shoulder.

Then – hurray! Pants. A pair of blue pants. What a wonderful sight.

Horrid Henry pulled the pants from the pile. Oh no. They were the teeniest, tiniest pair he'd ever seen. Some toddler must have lost them.

Rats, thought Horrid Henry. Well, no way was he wearing his horrible pink pants a second longer. He'd just have to trade pants with someone. And Horrid Henry had the perfect someone in mind.

Chapter 5

Henry found Peter in the playground
playing tag with Tidy Ted.
"I need to talk to you in private,"
said Henry. "It's urgent."
"What about?" said Peter cautiously.

"It's top secret," said Henry. Out of
the corner of his eye he saw Dave
and Toby sneaking towards him.
Top secret! Henry never shared top
secret secrets with Peter.

"Quick!" yelped Henry. "There's no
time to lose!"
He ducked into the boys' toilet.
Peter followed.

"Peter, I'm worried about you," said
Horrid Henry. He tried to look
concerned.
"I'm fine," said Peter.

"No you're not," said Henry. "I've
heard bad things about you."
"What bad things?" said Peter
anxiously. Not – not that he had run
across the carpet in class?

"Embarrassing rumours," said Horrid
Henry. "But if I don't tell you, who
will? After all," he said, putting his
arm around Peter's shoulder, "it's my
job to look after you. Big brothers
should look out for little ones."

Perfect Peter could not believe
his ears.
"Oh, Henry," said Peter.
"I've always wanted a brother who
looked after me."

"That's me," said Henry. "Now listen.
I've heard you wear baby pants."
"I do not," said Peter. "Look!" And
he showed Henry his Daffy and her
Dancing Daisies pants.

Horrid Henry's heart went cold.
Daffy and her Dancing Daisies!

Ugh.

Yuck.

Gross.

But even Daffy would be a million
billion times better than pink pants
with lace ruffles.

"Daffy Daisy are the most babyish pants you could wear," said Henry. "Worse than wearing a nappy. Everyone will tease you."

Peter's lip trembled. He hated being teased. "What can I do?" he asked.

Henry pretended to think. "Look.
I'll do you a big favour. I'll swap
my pants for
yours. That way
I'll get teased,
not you."

"Thank you,
Henry," said Peter.
"You're the best brother
in the world." Then he stopped.

"Wait a minute," he said suspiciously.
"Let's see your pants."
"Why?" said Henry.
"Because," said Peter, "how do
I know you've even got pants
to swap?"

Horrid Henry was outraged.
"Of course I've got pants,"
said Henry.
"Then show me," said Peter.

Horrid Henry was trapped.
"OK," he said, giving Peter
a quick flash of pink lace.

Perfect Peter stared at Henry's
underpants.
"Those are your pants?" he said.
"Sure," said Horrid Henry.
"These are big boy pants."

"But they're **pink**," said Peter.

"All big boys wear **pink**,"
said Henry.

"But they have *lace* on them,"
said Peter.

"All big boys' pants have *lace*,"
said Henry.

"But they have
hearts and bows,"
said Peter.

"Of course they do, they're big boy pants," said Horrid Henry. "You wouldn't know because you only wear baby pants."
Peter hesitated. "But . . . but . . . they look like - girls' pants," said Peter.

Henry snorted. "Girls' pants! Do you think I'd ever wear girls' pants? These are what all the cool kids are wearing. You'll be the coolest kid in the class in these."

Perfect Peter backed away.
"No I won't," said Peter.
"Yes you will," said Henry.
"I don't want to wear your smelly
pants," said Peter.
"They're not smelly," said Henry.
"They're brand new. Now give me
your pants."

"NO!" screamed Peter.

"YES!" screamed Henry.

"Give me your pants!"

138

"What's going on in here?" came a
voice of steel. It was the Head,
Mrs Oddbod.
"Nothing," said Henry.
"There's no hanging about the toilets
at playtime," said Mrs Oddbod.
"Out of here, both of you."

Peter ran out of the door.
Now what do I do, thought
Horrid Henry.

Henry ducked into a stall and hid
the pink pants on the ledge above
the third toilet.
No way was he putting those pants
back on. Better Henry no pants than
Henry pink pants.

Chapter 6

At lunchtime Horrid Henry dodged
Graham. He dodged Toby by the
climbing frame.

During last play Dave
almost caught him by
the water fountain but
Henry was too quick.

Ralph chased him into
class but Henry got to
his seat just in time.

He'd done it!

Only forty-five minutes to go until home time. There'd be no de-bagging after school with parents around.

Henry couldn't believe it. He was
safe at last.

He stuck out his tongue at Ralph.

Miss Battle-Axe clapped her claws.
"Time to change for P.E,"
said Miss Battle-Axe.

P.E! It couldn't be - not a P.E. day.
"And I don't care if aliens stole your
P.E. kit, Henry," said Miss Battle-Axe,
glaring at him. "No excuses."

That's what she thought. He had the
perfect excuse. Even a teacher as
mean and horrible as Miss Battle-Axe
would not force a boy to do P.E.
without pants. Horrid Henry went
up to Miss Battle-Axe and whispered
in her ear.

"Forgot your pants, eh?"
barked Miss Battle-Axe loudly.
Henry blushed scarlet. When he was
king he'd make Miss Battle-Axe walk
around town every day wearing pants
on her head.

"Well, Henry, today is your lucky
day," said Miss Battle-Axe, pulling
something pink and lacy out of her
pocket. "I found these in the boys'
toilets."

"Take them away!"

screamed Horrid Henry.

HORRID HENRY'S
Nits

Contents

This book is dedicated to William Gee who would like to thank all the boys in 2BC at The Hall School for being such great classmates:

Laurie Ashcroft
Gus Beagles
Angus Bloch
James Claydon
Nicholas Corbett
Luke Eadie
Alec Ezra
Max Fairfull
Jacob Goldberg
Cal Gorvy
Thomas Hocking
Boaz Lister
Phelim Owens
Tej Shah
Zaki Siddiqui
Nathaniel Swift
James Taylor

We would also like to thank the following teachers: Rebecca McDonald, Susie Wesson, Nicky Gill, Kirsty Anderson and of course Katie Bonham-Carter.

Chapter 1

Scratch. Scratch. Scratch.

Dad scratched his head.
"Stop scratching, please," said Mum.
"We're eating dinner."

Mum scratched her head.
"Stop scratching, please," said Dad.
"We're eating dinner."

Henry scratched his head.

"Stop scratching, Henry!"
said Mum and Dad.

"Uh-oh," said Mum. She put down
her fork and frowned at Henry.
"Henry, do you have nits *again*?"

"Of course not," said Henry.

"Come over to the sink, Henry,"
said Mum.

"Why?" said Henry.

"I need to check your head."

Henry dragged his feet over to her
as slowly as possible. It's not fair,
he thought.

It wasn't his fault nits loved him.
Henry's head was a gathering place
for nits far and wide. They probably
held nit parties there and foreign nits
visited him on their holidays.

Mum dragged the nit comb across
Henry's head. She made a face
and groaned.
"You're crawling with nits, Henry,"
said Mum.

"Ooh, let's see," said Henry.
He always liked counting
how many nits he had.

"One,

two,

three . . .

forty-five, forty-six,

forty-seven..."

he counted, dropping them
on to a paper towel.

"It's not polite to count nits,"
said his younger brother,
Perfect Peter, wiping his mouth
with his spotless napkin.
"Is it, Mum?"

"It certainly isn't," said Mum.

Chapter 2

Dad dragged the nit comb across
his head and made a face.
"Ughh," said Dad.

Mum dragged the comb through
her hair.
"Bleccch," said Mum.

Mum combed Perfect Peter's hair.
Then she did it again. And again.
And again.

"No nits, Peter," said Mum, smiling.
"As usual. Well done, darling."
Perfect Peter smiled modestly.
"It's because I wash and comb my
hair every night," said Peter.

Henry scowled. True, his hair was
filthy, but then . . .
"Nits love clean hair," said Henry.

"No they don't," said Peter.
"*I've* never ever had nits."

We'll see about that, thought Henry.

When no one was looking he picked
a few nits off the paper towel.
Then he wandered over to Peter and
casually fingered a lock of his hair.

LEAP!

Scratch.

Scratch.

"Mum!" squealed Peter. "Henry's
pulling my hair!"

"Stop it, Henry," said Dad.

"I wasn't pulling his hair,"
said Henry indignantly.
"I just wanted to see how clean
it was. And it *is* so lovely and clean,"
added Henry sweetly.
"I wish my hair was as clean as Peter's."

Peter beamed. It wasn't often that
Henry said anything nice to him.

"Right," said Mum grimly, "everyone
upstairs. It's shampoo time."

Chapter 3

"NO!" shrieked Horrid Henry.

"NO SHAMPOO!"

He hated the stinky smelly horrible shampoo much more than he hated having nits. Only today his teacher, Miss Battle-Axe, had sent home a nit letter.

BEWARE!
Nits Nits Nits Nits

Nits have been seen in school.

GET RID OF THEM!

Wash your hair with supersonic NIT Blasting Shampoo

PLEASE . . .

OR ELSE.

Naturally, Henry had crumpled
the letter and thrown it away.
He was never ever going to have
pongy nit shampoo on his head
again. What rotten luck Mum had
spotted him scratching.

"It's the only way to get rid of nits," said Dad.

"But it never works!" screamed Henry. And he ran for the door. Mum and Dad grabbed him. Then they dragged him kicking and screaming to the bathroom.

"Nits are living creatures,"
howled Henry. "Why kill them?"

"Because..." said Mum.

"Because ... because ... they're
blood-sucking nits," said Dad.

Blood-sucking.

Henry had never thought of that.

In the split second that he stood
still to consider this interesting
information, Mum emptied the
bottle of supersonic nit-blasting
shampoo over his hair.
"NO!" screamed Henry.
Frantically he shook his head.

There was shampoo on the door.
There was shampoo on the floor.
There was shampoo all over
Mum and Dad.
The only place there was
no shampoo was on Henry's head.
"Henry! Stop being horrid!" yelled
Dad, wiping shampoo off his jacket.

"What a big fuss over nothing,"
said Peter.
Henry lunged at him.
Mum seized Henry by the collar
and held him back.

"Now, Peter," said Mum. "That wasn't
a kind thing to say to Henry, was it?
Not everyone is as brave as you."

176

"You're right, Mum," said Perfect Peter. "I was being rude and thoughtless. It won't happen again. I'm so sorry, Henry."

Mum smiled at him. "That was a perfect apology, Peter. As for you, Henry . . ." she sighed. "We'll get more shampoo tomorrow."

Phew, thought Henry, giving
his head an extra good scratch.
Safe for one more day.

Chapter 4

The next morning at school a group
of parents burst into the classroom,
waving the nit letter and shouting.

My Margaret doesn't have nits! She never has and she never will. How dare you send home such a letter!

shrieked Moody Margaret's mother.

The idea! My Josh doesn't have nits,

shouted his mother.

My Toby doesn't have nits! Some nasty child in this class isn't bug-busting!

shouted his father.

Miss Battle-Axe squared her
shoulders.
"Rest assured that the culprit
will be found," she said.
"I have declared war on nits."

Scratch. Scratch. Scratch.

Miss Battle-Axe spun round.
Her beady eyes swivelled
over the class.
"Who's scratching?" she demanded.

Silence.

Henry bent over his worksheet and
tried to look studious.
"Henry is," said Moody Margaret.

"Liar!" shouted Horrid Henry.
"It was William!"
Weepy William burst into tears.
"No it wasn't," he sobbed.

Miss Battle-Axe glared at the class.
"I'm going to find out once and for
all who's got nits," she growled.

"Silence!" ordered Miss Battle-Axe. "Nora, the nit nurse, is coming this morning. Who's got nits? Who's not bug-busting? We'll all find out soon."

Uh-oh, thought Henry.
Now I'm sunk.

There was no escaping Nitty Nora
Bug Explorer and her ferocious
combs. **Everyone** would know
he had the nits.

Rude Ralph would never
stop teasing him.

He'd be shampooed every night.

Mum and Dad would find out
about all the nit letters he'd
thrown away . . .

He could of course get a tummy
ache double quick and be sent home.
But Nitty Nora had a horrible way
of remembering whose head she
hadn't checked and then combing
it in front of the whole class.

He could run screaming out of the door saying he'd caught mad cow disease. But somehow he didn't think Miss Battle-Axe would believe him.

There was no way out. This time he was well and truly stuck.

Unless . . .
Suddenly Henry had a wonderful,
spectacular idea.

It was so wicked, and so horrible,
that even Horrid Henry hesitated.

But only for a moment.
Desperate times call for desperate
measures.

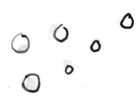

Chapter 5

Henry leaned over Clever Clare and brushed his head lightly against hers.

LEAP!

Scratch. *Scratch.*

"Get away from me, Henry,"
hissed Clare.
"I was just admiring your lovely
picture," said Henry.

He got up to sharpen his pencil.
On his way to the sharpener he
brushed against Greedy Graham.

LEAP!

Scratch. Scratch.

On his way back from the sharpener
Henry stumbled and fell against
Anxious Andrew.

LEAP!

Scratch.

Scratch.

"Ow!" yelped Andrew.
"Sorry, Andrew," said Henry.
"What big clumsy feet I have."

"Whoops!" he added, tripping over
the carpet and banging heads
with Weepy William.

LEAP!

Scratch.

Scratch.

"Waaaaaaaaa!" wailed William.
"Sit down at once, Henry,"
said Miss Battle-Axe.
"William! Stop scratching.
Bert! How do you spell cat?"

"I dunno," said Beefy Bert.
Horrid Henry leaned across the table
and put his head close to Bert's.
"C–A–T," he whispered helpfully.

LEAP!

Scratch.

Scratch.

Then Horrid Henry raised his hand.
"Yes?" said Miss Battle-Axe.
"I don't understand these
instructions," said Henry sweetly.
"Could you help me, please?"

Miss Battle-Axe frowned.
She liked to keep as far away from
Henry as possible. Reluctantly she
came closer and bent over his work.

Henry leaned his head near hers.

 LEAP!

Scratch.

 Scratch.

Chapter 6

There was a pounding at the door.
Then Nitty Nora marched into the
classroom, bristling with combs and
other instruments of torture.

"Line up, everyone,"
said Miss Battle-Axe, patting her hair.
"The nit nurse is here."

Rats, thought Henry.
He'd hardly started.
Slowly, he stood up.

Everyone pushed and shoved to be
first in line. Then a few children
remembered what they were
lining up for and stampeded
towards the back.

Horrid Henry saw his chance
and took it.
He charged through the squabbling
children, brushing against everyone
as fast as he could.

LEAP!

Scratch! Scratch!

LEAP!

Scratch!

Scratch!

LEAP!

Scratch!

Scratch!

"Henry!" shouted Miss Battle-Axe.
"Stay in at playtime. Now go to the
end of the queue. The rest of you,
stop this nonsense at once!"

202

Moody Margaret had fought longest
and hardest to be first. Proudly she
presented her head to Nitty Nora.
"I certainly don't have nits," she said.

Nitty Nora stuck the comb in.

"Nits!"

she announced, stuffing a nit note
into Margaret's hand.
For once Margaret was too shocked
to speak.

"But . . . but . . ." she gasped.

Tee-hee, thought Henry.
Now he wouldn't be the only one.

"Next," said Nitty Nora.
She stuck the comb in
Rude Ralph's greasy hair.

"Nits!" she announced.

"Nit-face," hissed Horrid Henry,
beside himself with glee.

"Nits!" said Nitty Nora,
poking her comb into
Lazy Linda's mop.

"Nits!"

said Nitty Nora, prodding Greedy
Graham's frizzy hair.

"Nits, nits, nits, nits, nits!"

she continued, pointing at
Weepy William, Clever Clare,
Sour Susan, Beefy Bert and
Dizzy Dave.

Then Nitty Nora beckoned to
Miss Battle-Axe.
"Teachers too," she ordered.

Miss Battle-Axe's jaw dropped.
"I have been teaching for twenty-five
years and I have never had nits,"
she said. "Don't waste your time
checking *me*."

Nitty Nora ignored her protests
and stuck in the comb.
"Hmmn," she said, and whispered
in Miss Battle-Axe's ear.

"NO"

howled Miss Battle-Axe.

"NOOOOOOOOOO!"

Then she joined the line of
weeping, wailing children clutching
their nit notes.

At last it was Henry's turn.
Nitty Nora stuck her comb into
Henry's tangled hair and dragged it
across his scalp. She combed again.
And again. And again.

"No nits," said Nitty Nora.
"Keep up the good work,
young man."
"I sure will!" said Henry.

Horrid Henry skipped home
waving his certificate.
"Look, Peter," crowed Henry.
"I'm nit-free!"
Perfect Peter burst into tears.
"I'm not," he wailed.

"Hard luck," said Horrid Henry.

HORRiD HENRY
and the
Football Fiend

Contents

For Amanda Craig

Chapter 1

"…AND with 15 seconds to go
it's Hot-Foot Henry racing across
the pitch!

Rooney tries a slide tackle
but Henry's too quick!

Just look at that step-over!

Oh no, he can't score from
that distance,

.   it's **crazy**

it's **impossible**

oh my goodness,
he cornered the ball. . .

it's IN!!!! It's IN!

Another spectacular win!
And it's all thanks to Hot-Foot
Henry, the greatest footballer
who's ever lived!"

"Goal! Goal! Goal!"
roared the crowd.

Hot-Foot Henry had won the match!
His teammates carried him through
the fans, cheering and chanting,
"Hen-ry! Hen-ry! Hen-ry!"

"HENRY!"

Horrid Henry looked up to see Miss
Battle-Axe leaning over his table and
glaring at him with her red eyes.
"What did I just say?"

"Henry," said Horrid Henry.
Miss Battle-Axe scowled.
"I'm watching you, Henry," she
snapped. "Now class, please pay
attention, we need to discuss—"

"Waaaaa!"
wailed Weepy William.

"Susan, stop pulling
my hair!"
squealed Vain Violet.

"Miss!"
shouted Inky Ian.
"Ralph's snatched
my pen!"

"Didn't!"
shouted Rude Ralph.

"Did!"
shouted Inky Ian.

"Class! Be quiet!"
bellowed Miss Battle-Axe.

"Waaaaa!"

wailed Weepy William.

"Owwww!"

squealed Vain Violet.

"Give it back!"

shouted Inky Ian.

"Fine," said Miss Battle-Axe,
"we won't talk about football."

William stopped wailing.
Violet stopped squealing.
Ian stopped shouting.
Henry stopped daydreaming.

Everyone in the class stared at
Miss Battle-Axe.

Chapter 2

Miss Battle-Axe wanted to talk about
... football?
Was this an alien Miss Battle-Axe?

"As you all know, our local team,
Ashton Athletic, has reached the
sixth round of the FA Cup,"
said Miss Battle-Axe.
"YAY!" shrieked the class.

"And I'm sure you all know what
happened last night…"

Last night!

Henry could still hear the announcer's
glorious words as
he and Peter had gathered round
the radio as the draw for
round six was announced.

"Number 16, Ashton Athletic, will be playing…" There was a long pause as the announcer drew another ball from the hat… "number 7, Manchester United."
"Go Ashton!" shrieked Horrid Henry.

"As I was saying, before I was so rudely interrupted…" Miss Battle-Axe glared at Horrid Henry.

"Ashton are playing Manchester United in a few weeks. Every local primary school has been given a pair of tickets. And thanks to my good luck in the teachers' draw, the lucky winner will come from our class."

"Me!" screamed Horrid Henry.
"Me!" screamed Moody Margaret.
"Me!" screamed Tough Toby, Aerobic Al, Fiery Fiona and Brainy Brian.

"No one who shouts out
will be getting anything," said Miss
Battle-Axe. "Our class will be playing
a football match at lunchtime.
The player of the match will win
the tickets. I'm the referee and my
decision will be final."

Chapter 3

Horrid Henry was so stunned that
for a moment he could scarcely
breathe. FA Cup tickets! FA Cup
tickets to see his local team
Ashton play against Man U!
Those tickets were like gold dust.

Henry had begged and pleaded
with Mum and Dad to get tickets,
but naturally they were all sold out
by the time Henry's mean, horrible,
lazy parents managed to heave their
stupid bones to the phone.

And now here was another chance
to go to the match of the century!

Ashton Athletic had never got
so far in the Cup.
Sure, they'd knocked out the

Tooting Tigers
(chant: Toot Toot! Grrr!),

the **Pynchley Pythons**
and the **Cheam Champions**

but – **Manchester United!**

Henry had to go to the game.
He just had to. And all he had to do
was be man of the match.

There was just one problem.
Unfortunately, the best footballer
in the class wasn't

~~Horrid Henry.~~

~~Or Aerobic Al.~~

~~Or Beefy Bert.~~

The **best footballer** in the class was Moody Margaret.

The **second best** player in the class was Moody Margaret.

The **third best** player in the class was Moody Margaret.

It was **so** unfair!

Why should Margaret of all people
be so fantastic at football?

Horrid Henry was brilliant
at shirt pulling.

Horrid Henry was superb
at screaming "Offside!"
(whatever that meant).

No one could howl
"Come on, ref!" louder.

And at

toe-treading,

 elbowing,

barging,

pushing,

 shoving

and

tripping,

Horrid Henry had no equal.

The only thing Horrid Henry wasn't good at was playing football.

243

But never mind.
Today would be different.
Today he would dig deep inside
and find the power to be

Hot-Foot Henry

– for real.
Today no one would stop him.
FA Cup match here I come,
thought Henry gleefully.

Chapter 4

Lunchtime!

Horrid Henry's class dashed to
the back playground where the pitch
was set up. Two jumpers either end
marked the goals. A few parents
gathered on the sidelines.

Miss Battle-Axe split the class into
two teams: Aerobic Al was captain of
Henry's team, Moody Margaret was
captain of the other.

There she stood in midfield, having
nabbed a striker position, smirking
confidently. Horrid Henry glared at
her from the depths of the outfield.

"Na na ne nah nah,

I'm sure to be man of the match,"
trilled Moody Margaret,
sticking out her tongue at him.
"and you-ooo won't."

"Shut up, Margaret," said Henry.
When he was king, anyone named
Margaret would be boiled in oil
and fed to the crows.

"Will you take me to the match,
Margaret?" said Susan.
"After all, *I'm* your best friend."

Moody Margaret scowled.
"Since when?"
"Since always!" wailed Susan.
"Huh!" said Margaret.
"We'll just have to see how nice
you are to me, won't we?"

"Take me,"

begged Brainy Brian.

"Remember how I helped you
with those fractions?"

"And called me **stupid,**"

said Margaret.

"Didn't," said Brian.

"Did," said Margaret.

Horrid Henry eyed his classmates.
Everyone looking straight ahead,
everyone determined to be man
of the match.

Well, wouldn't they be in for a shock
when Horrid Henry waltzed off
with those tickets!

Chapter 5

screeched
Moody Margaret's mum.

screeched
Aerobic Al's dad.

"Everyone ready?" said
Miss Battle-Axe.
"Bert! Which team are you on?"

"I dunno," said Beefy Bert.

Miss Battle-Axe blew her whistle.

Kick-off!

Kick.

Chase.

Kick

Dribble.

Dribble.

Pass.

Kick.

Save!

Goal kick.

Henry stood disconsolately on the
left wing, running back and forth
as the play passed him by.
How could he ever be man of the
match stuck out here? Well, no way
was he staying in this stupid spot
a moment longer.

Horrid Henry abandoned his
position and chased after the ball.
All the other defenders followed him.

Moody Margaret had the ball.
Horrid Henry ran up behind her.

He glanced at Miss Battle-Axe.
She was busy chatting to
Mrs Oddbod.
Horrid Henry went for a two foot
slide tackle and tripped her.

"Cheater!"
screamed Moody Margaret's
mum.

"Play on,"
ordered Miss Battle-Axe.
Yes! thought Henry triumphantly.
After all, what did blind old
Miss Battle-Axe know about
the rules of football?

Nothing.

This was his golden chance to score.
Now Jazzy Jim had the ball.

Horrid Henry trod on his toes,
elbowed him, and grabbed the ball.

"Hey, we're on the same team!"
yelped Jim.
Horrid Henry kept dribbling.
"Pass! Pass!" screamed Al. "Man on!"

Henry ignored him. Pass the ball?
Was Al mad? For once Henry had
the ball and he was keeping it.

Then suddenly Moody Margaret
appeared from behind, barged him,
dribbled the ball past Henry's team
and kicked it straight past
Weepy William into goal.

Moody Margaret's team cheered.
Weepy William burst into tears.

"Waaaaaa,"

wailed Weepy William.

"Idiot!"

screamed Aerobic Al's dad.

"She cheated!
She fouled me!"

shrieked Henry.

"Didn't"

said Margaret.

"How dare you call my daughter a cheater?" screamed Moody Margaret's mum.

Miss Battle-Axe blew her whistle.
"Goal to Margaret's team.
The score is one-nil."

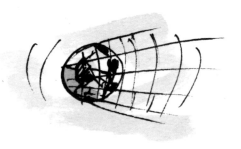

Chapter 6

Horrid Henry gritted his teeth.
He would score a goal if he had to
trample on every player to do so.
Unfortunately, everyone else seemed
to have the same idea.

"Ralph pushed me!"
shrieked Aerobic Al.
"Didn't," lied Rude Ralph.
"It was just a barge."

"He used his hands, I saw him!"
howled Al's father. "Send him off."
"I'll send *you* off if you don't
behave," snapped Miss Battle-Axe,
looking up and blowing her whistle.

"It was kept in!"
protested Henry.

"No way!" shouted Margaret.
"It went past the line!"

"That was ball to hand!"
yelled Kind Kasim.

"No way!" screamed Aerobic Al.
"I just went for the ball."

"Free kick to Margaret's team,"
said Miss Battle-Axe.
"Ouch!" screamed Soraya, as Brian
stepped on her toes, grabbed the ball,
and headed it into goal past Kasim.

"Hurray!" cheered Al's team.
"Foul!" screamed Margaret's team.

"Score is one all," said Miss
Battle-Axe. "Five more minutes
to go."

AAARRRGGHH!

thought Horrid Henry.
I've got to score a goal to have
a chance to be man of the match.
I've just got to. But how, how?

Henry glanced at Miss Battle-Axe.
She appeared to be rummaging in
her handbag.

Henry saw his chance. He stuck out
his foot as Margaret hurtled past.

Crash!

Margaret tumbled.
Henry seized the ball.

Henry hacked
my leg!

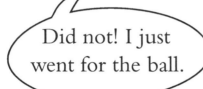

Did not! I just
went for the ball.

"REF!"

screamed Margaret.

"He cheated!" screamed Margaret's
mum. "Are you blind, ref?"

Miss Battle-Axe glared.
"My eyesight is perfect, thank you,"
she snapped.
Tee hee, chortled Horrid Henry.

Henry trod on Brian's toes, elbowed
him, then grabbed the ball.

Then Dave elbowed Henry,
Ralph trod on Dave's toes, and
Susan seized the ball and kicked it
high overhead.

Henry looked up.
The ball was high, high up.
He'd never reach it, not unless,
unless—

Henry glanced at Miss Battle-Axe.
She was watching a traffic warden
patrolling outside the school gate.
Henry leapt into the air and whacked
the ball with his hand.

Thwack!

The ball hurled across the goal.

"Goal!" screamed Henry.

"He used his hands!"
protested Margaret.

"No way!" shouted Henry.
"It was the hand of God!"

"Hen–ry! Hen–ry! Hen–ry!"

cheered his team.

"Unfair!"

howled Margaret's team.

Miss Battle-Axe blew her whistle.
"Time!" she bellowed.
"Al's team wins 2-1."
"Yes!" shrieked Horrid Henry,
punching the air. He'd scored the
winning goal! He'd be man of the
match! Ashton Athletic versus
Man U here I come!

Horrid Henry's class limped
through the door and sat down.
Horrid Henry sat at the front,
beaming.

Miss Battle-Axe had to award him
the tickets after his brilliant
performance and spectacular,
game-winning goal.

The question was, who *deserved*
to be his guest?

No one.

I know, thought Horrid Henry,
I'll sell my other ticket. Bet I get a
million pounds for it. No, a billion
pounds.

Then I'll buy my own football team,
and play striker any time I want to.
Horrid Henry smiled happily.

Miss Battle-Axe glared at her class.
"That was absolutely disgraceful," she
said. "Cheating! Moving the goals!
Shirt tugging!"
She glared at Graham. "Barging!"
She glowered at Ralph. "Pushing and
shoving! Bad sportsmanship!"

Her eyes swept over the class.
Horrid Henry sank lower in his seat.

Oops.

"And don't get me started about
offside," she snapped.

Horrid Henry sank even lower.
"There was only one person
who deserved to be player of the
match," she continued.
"One person who observed the rules
of the beautiful game…
One person who has nothing
to be ashamed of today…"

Horrid Henry's heart leapt.
He certainly had nothing
to be ashamed of.

"…One person who can truly
be proud of their performance…"
Horrid Henry beamed with pride.
"And that person is—"

"Me!"

screamed Moody Margaret.

"Me!"

screamed Aerobic Al.

"Me!"

screamed Horrid Henry.

"—the referee," said Miss Battle-Axe.

What?

Miss Battle-Axe … man of the match?

Miss Battle-Axe … a football fiend?

"IT'S NOT FAIR!"
screamed the class.

"IT'S NOT FAIR!"

screamed Horrid Henry.

HORRID HENRY

by Francesca Simon

Illustrated by Tony Ross

Paperbacks with four stories each

Horrid Henry

Horrid Henry and the Secret Club

Horrid Henry Tricks the Tooth Fairy

Horrid Henry's Nits

Horrid Henry Gets Rich Quick

Horrid Henry's Haunted House

Horrid Henry and the Mummy's Curse

Horrid Henry's Revenge

Horrid Henry and the Bogey Babysitter

Horrid Henry's Stinkbomb

Horrid Henry's Underpants

Horrid Henry Meets the Queen

Horrid Henry and the Mega-Mean Time Machine

Horrid Henry and the Football Fiend

Horrid Henry's Christmas Cracker

Horrid Henry and the Abominable Snowman

Horrid Henry Robs the Bank

Horrid Henry Wakes the Dead

Horrid Henry Rocks
Horrid Henry and the Zombie Vampire
Horrid Henry's Monster Movie

Early Readers

Don't Be Horrid, Henry!
Horrid Henry's Birthday Party
Horrid Henry's Holiday
Horrid Henry's Underpants
Horrid Henry Gets Rich Quick
Horrid Henry and the Football Fiend
Horrid Henry's Nits
Horrid Henry and Moody Margaret
Horrid Henry's Thank You Letter
Horrid Henry Reads a Book
Horrid Henry's Car Journey
Moody Margaret's School
Horrid Henry Tricks and Treats
Horrid Henry's Christmas Play
Horrid Henry's Rainy Day
Horrid Henry's Author Visit
Horrid Henry Meets the Queen
Horrid Henry's Sports Day
Moody Margaret Casts a Spell
Horrid Henry's Christmas Presents

Big colour collections

Horrid Henry's Big Bad Book
Horrid Henry's Wicked Ways
Horrid Henry's Evil Enemies
Horrid Henry Rules the World
Horrid Henry's House of Horrors
Horrid Henry's Dreadful Deeds
Horrid Henry Shows Who's Boss
Horrid Henry's A–Z of Everything Horrid

Joke Books

Horrid Henry's Joke Book
Horrid Henry's Jolly Joke Book
Horrid Henry's Mighty Joke Book
Horrid Henry versus Moody Margaret
Horrid Henry's Hilariously Horrid Joke Book
Horrid Henry's All Time Favourite Joke Book

Extra books

Horrid Henry's Annual 2013

Visit Horrid Henry's website at
www.horridhenry.co.uk for competitions,
games, downloads and a monthly newsletter!